Boobela
and
Worm

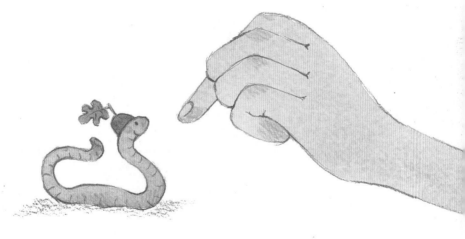

First published in Great Britain in 2007
by Orion Children's Books
a division of the Orion Publishing Group Ltd
Orion House
5 Upper St Martin's Lane
London WC2H 9EA
An Hachette Livre UK Company

3 5 7 9 10 8 6 4 2

Text copyright © Joe Friedman 2007
Illustrations copyright © Sam Childs 2007

Design by Sarah Hodder

The rights of Joe Friedman and Sam Childs to be identified as the author and illustrator of this work
respectively have been asserted.

A catalogue record for this book is available from the British Library.

Printed and bound in Italy by Printer Trento

ISBN 978 1 84255 539 2

Boobela
and
Worm

Joe Friedman

illustrated by Sam Childs

Orion
Children's Books

Contents

Between each story, you can discover more about Boobela and Worm and the world they live in.

To my daughter Susie,
who loves bedtime stories.
J.F.

To Helena Gavshon, the fabric queen
and to Joan and Freddie Lavender,
whose passion for children's books
is unsurpassed.
S.C.

Boobela Meets Worm

"Your feet stink."

Boobela looked around. She couldn't see anyone. Then she heard the little voice again.

"Your feet stink."

Boobela was very surprised. No one ever talked to her, and *no one* ever said anything nasty to her. Most of the time people just ran away.

Boobela was a young giant. Everyone was scared of her. Everyone except, it seemed, the owner of this little voice.

Boobela looked closely at the ground near her feet. She saw a worm with his head sticking out of the ground.

"Isn't it usual," said the worm, "to reply when you are spoken to?"

Boobela nodded.

"Let's start again," said the worm. "Your feet stink. Your turn."

Boobela said, "I forgot to wash them this week. Or last."

"Or the week before, from the smell of them," replied the worm.

"I didn't think . . ." said Boobela.

"Anybody cared?"
asked the worm softly.
Boobela nodded a
very small nod.

She was
beginning to get
over the shock of
speaking to someone.
Especially a worm. It
was rather a nice shock.

"I'm Boobela," she began.
"What's your name?"

"That's more like it," said
the worm. "I'm Worm."

"Don't you have a name, like
Jamie or Daniel?" asked Boobela.
The worm's head and body
shook. "A worm called Jamie?"
he said, laughing so hard he
was barely able to speak.
"That would be too silly.

We worms don't put on airs. We're all called Worm."

"Why aren't you scared of me?"

"Why should I be?" said Worm.

"I'm much bigger than you," said Boobela.

"Silly billy," said Worm, "everything is bigger than me. If I was scared to speak to anyone bigger than me, I'd have a very quiet time of it."

Boobela took a deep breath. "Would you come to my house for tea?" she asked.

"All right," said Worm. "Tomorrow. Meet me right here, at four." Worm looked around. "I hope your house is tidier than your garden."

Worm burrowed into the ground and, in a moment, was gone.

Boobela looked around her. She had never thought of her garden as untidy. But she could see what Worm meant.

Where there was grass, it was up to her knees. Mostly, there were weeds. Weeds, empty crisp packets and chocolate wrappers.

Boobela suddenly felt ashamed. She hadn't thought of all the garden creatures having to live in this mess.

She went inside.

If anything, Boobela's house was a bigger mess than her garden. There were biscuit crumbs, stacks of old newspapers and dirty clothes, empty tins, and dirty cups and plates. Everywhere. The plates were so slimy even mice avoided them. Worm would hate it!

That night and the following day, Boobela was a whirlwind of activity. She cleaned and tidied her house and washed herself from head to toe – particularly her toes – several times. She cut the grass in her garden and cleared up all the old wrappers and tins.

When she'd finished, she made her favourite
banana cake for tea. She put on her best clothes:
a new T-shirt with a picture of a rainbow on it, jeans
with only one hole and her prized baseball cap.
Then she sat down to have a little rest.

Suddenly, Boobela realised with a terrible shock
that worms probably don't like banana cake. What
could she give him for tea? Who could she ask?

Boobela remembered a lovely garden she had
seen once. Maybe the gardener would know what
worms ate. She hurried to his garden. To her

surprise, the gardener simply
watched as she came near.

"You didn't run away,"
she said.

The gardener looked sad.
"My running days are over,
big 'un." He paused. "You
look like you're in trouble. "

Boobela's feelings just rushed out. "I have a worm coming over for tea and I want him to like me but I don't know what to give him because I don't know what worms eat and I don't think he'd like banana cake."

The gardener paused to think.

"Worms . . . they don't travel much," he said. "So, he'd probably like soil from another garden. Maybe you could make him a mud pie."

"I'd love that!" said Boobela. "But where would I go to find the soil?"

The gardener said, "Wait here." He turned and went into his house. He was bent over and moved very slowly. Boobela could see he was in pain.

The gardener came out of his house with a plate. Moving slowly, he filled it with three different kinds of soil from his garden. He handed the plate to Boobela. "This should be a real treat for your worm."

"Thank you. Thank you," said Boobela, who was so happy she felt like crying. It had been such a long time since anyone had been kind to her.

Boobela started for home. She wished she could do something for the gardener in return for his help. Suddenly, Boobela became aware of a tingling in her hands. They felt very warm. Boobela wasn't sure what was happening.

She raised her hands and pointed them at the gardener. To her surprise, she felt the tingling and warmth get stronger.

The gardener suddenly stood up straight. He looked very surprised. He took a step and another. Then he danced a little jig. "My pain has gone!" he shouted.

Boobela looked at
her hands. She didn't
really understand what
had happened, but she
knew it was good.

As she walked, her head
was full of thoughts. Since
she'd met Worm, her whole life
had changed. And now something
special had happened. Maybe I have
magic inside me, Boobela thought.

In the kitchen, Boobela put the soil on a
plate and made a lovely mud pie. Then she placed
a shiny metal cover over it and put it on the
kitchen table. She washed her hands. Twice.

She went to fetch Worm. He stuck his head out
of the ground at exactly four o'clock. He looked
around him at the garden.

"You've been busy," he noted, approvingly.

Boobela carefully scooped up the soil around Worm, and carried him into her house.

She put him down on the kitchen table. Worm crawled around and saw the banana cake. He then inspected the rest of the table.

"What's under here?" he asked.

Boobela smiled. "I thought you'd never ask!" She lifted the cover with a flourish.

Worm crawled onto the plate and burrowed into the mud cake.

When he came out, a bit of leaf was stuck to his head. It looked like a hat.

"Isn't it usual to say thank you when a special treat is offered?" said Boobela.

Worm looked at Boobela closely, and then his whole body shook with laughter. "I think I'm going to like you."

They had a lovely tea. They talked and talked.

Boobela told Worm about how everybody ran away from her – although she wouldn't hurt a fly – and how sad that made her feel.

Worm asked, "Who do you live with?"

"I'm all by myself," replied Boobela.

"Why?"

"My parents went to the Dabushta Jungle to look for plants to make new medicines. My gran was looking after me, but then my granpa got ill and she had to go back to the little island where they live."

Worm looked at Boobela sympathetically. He could only imagine what it was like living alone. Being a worm meant he had hundreds of relatives living nearby.

Boobela ate her banana cake, and Worm burrowed all over the mud pie.

"That was delicious," he said. "I had no idea soils could taste so different, and so good."

This was the moment Boobela was waiting for. "If you were my friend," she said, "I could carry you around with me and you could have lovely mud pies wherever we went."

Worm smacked his lips at the thought. "And you?"

"I'd have a good friend who wasn't scared of me and would tell me the truth," said Boobela. "Ever since I met you my life has been better and I don't want us ever to part."

Worm thought. Then he smiled. "Me, neither."

"I've got something else for you." Boobela took out a small container she'd made from a large box of matches. It had a leather strap glued to it. Inside the box was the lovely dark soil. Worm inspected the box and climbed in.

Boobela lifted it and attached it to her shoulder. "This is brilliant," said Worm. From his new home, Worm could see the world and talk to Boobela as she walked around.

"When I first met you, I thought anybody who had such stinky feet must be selfish."

"I didn't have anybody to care about," said Boobela. "But now I have you."

Boobela and Worm's Wardrobe

I love clothes. But I hate washing them!
Since I met Worm, I've organised my
wardrobe. And I wash my clothes regularly.

I can't just go into a shop and
buy clothes, so I make my own.
I also pick and mix. I find
things that fit me and put
them together in ways that
I like. Here are some of my
favourites ...

singlet top

sparkly top

flower T-shirt

shorts

sash

sandals

tutu

leggings

22

extra-large baseball cap
(given to me by my Uncle Neill)

Worms don't wear clothes.
They'd just get in the way
when we're tunnelling
through the earth. But I
spend a lot of time above
ground with my friend
Boobela, so I need to be
protected from the sun.
Here are a few of the
hats I love best ...

cowboy hat

leaf hat

acorn hat

baseball hat

"Air Worm" cap

At the Seaside

Boobela strode along the empty
road. It was still dark. She was wearing
bright red shorts, her favourite rainbow
T-shirt, freshly washed, and had a purple

rucksack on her back. It held a large picnic lunch for herself and a mud pie for Worm. Worm was standing in his matchbox on her shoulder.

"What were you doing so late last night?" Worm asked, casually.

"It's a surprise," said Boobela, equally casually.

"A surprise for me?"

"If I said, it wouldn't be a surprise," said Boobela.

Worm thought about this. It sounded good. "You promise you'll keep an eye out for water . . ."

Worm had explained to Boobela that he was very, very afraid of two things: water and birds. Water because worms can drown in the earth if it's too wet. And birds because they love to eat worms.

"Don't be daft. We're going to the beach," said Boobela. "Of course there will be water."

"You know what I mean!" said Worm.

"The last thing I want is for you to be in danger," said Boobela.

• • •

"Look!" said Boobela.

She pointed to a sign saying "Herne Beach Two Miles".

They hurried along in the morning sunshine, catching glimpses of the sea. Soon, they saw the long, sandy beach. It was surrounded by arcades and fish and chip shops, but they didn't really notice. They stared at the sea.

Worm shuddered. "This is a worm's worst nightmare," he said. "I'll have to tell my mum and dad about this!"

Boobela was quiet. She was thinking that her mum and dad were far away, beyond a sea much larger than the one she was looking at.

"I shouldn't have said that," said Worm. "You must really miss your mum and dad."

Boobela nodded.

"Let's go and look at the arcades," said Worm.

Boobela shook her head. Her eyes were fixed on the children playing on the beach. She wanted to play with them. But she was afraid they wouldn't want to play with her.

"I'm too big," she said.

"You're not too anything," said Worm, "except too scared."

"Why would they want to play with me," asked Boobela, "when they could play with someone their own size?"

"They can play with people their own size all the time. Today will be their first chance to play with a giant!" said Worm. "Now, use your head and figure out something they can do only with you."

Boobela looked at the people on the beach.

Some were playing football, some volleyball. Some were building sandcastles. Then she saw a little girl being buried in the sand.

"I've got an idea!" said Boobela. "But first things first."

She put down her rucksack and fished out a little package. She opened it and took out a yellow Worm-sized cowboy hat. She'd made it the night before.

She fitted it on Worm's head. "To protect you from the sun," she said.

Worm loved the hat. He stood straight up, and stuck out his chest. "Pardner, am I cool or what?" he said. He sounded like a cowboy.

Whooping with laughter, Boobela picked up her rucksack and charged down to the water. She kicked off her shoes, and stepped in.

"Not deep," said Worm, anxiously.

"Just a paddle," said Boobela. "It's cold . . . but lovely."

On even the busiest beach day, a laughing giant running down to the sea is bound to attract some attention. A worm in a cowboy hat on her shoulder adds to the effect. Soon Boobela and Worm were surrounded by a large group of children. They stayed a safe distance away. They weren't sure what kind of giant Boobela was – a scary giant, or a friendly one.

Boobela took a deep breath. She'd been scared of approaching the gardener – and when she did, she'd discovered the magic in her. She'd be brave now too! "Showtime," she said, under her breath to Worm.

"Let's round up those kids, pardner," said Worm, in his cowboy voice.

Boobela couldn't giggle and be scared at the same time. She giggled. She turned to the children and said, "I bet you've never buried a giant before!"

The children looked at each other. She was right! "Bury the giant!" one shouted.

"Bury the giant!" another took up the cry.

In a moment, "Bury the giant!" rang out over the beach. More children ran towards Boobela.

In another moment, Boobela was lying on the sand, surrounded by children. Each had a shovel and was working hard to cover her with sand.

"We'll never do it," said a little girl called Cheryl. She was wearing a red sun hat with flowers on it.

"Of course we will," said her big brother, Simon. "There are loads of us!"

As the sand piled up onto Boobela's chest, Worm crawled up her neck to her head.

The children couldn't believe Boobela was only eight years old. "You're bigger than my dad," said Cheryl. "I wish I was that big!"

Boobela was buried right up to
her head. The children did a victory
war dance around the buried giant.
Several adults took photos.

"Let's make a sandcastle!" said Boobela.
A sand city!" said Worm.

"But you can't move, Boobela!" chorused
the children.

Boobela pretended to struggle,
grunting with effort. The
children laughed with
pleasure.

"I'll help you!" said
Cheryl. She got down
on her hands and knees
and used her shovel to push sand off
Boobela. She winked at the giant.

"We girls have to stick together."

Other girls joined in. Soon,
enough sand had been
removed for Boobela
to get up.

She shook off the
remaining sand.
The girls cheered.
"Where's our sandcastle
team?" asked Boobela.

All the children raised their hands.

"Just one thing," said Boobela. "We can't make
it too close to the water. Worm doesn't like water."

"What about right here?" asked a little boy.

Boobela and Worm looked at the water. It was
closer than before but still seemed a safe distance
away.

Worm nodded.

"Fine," said Boobela.

Simon took charge and organised the children into different teams. Some were to build a huge tower, some a city, some the walls around it, and some a moat around everything.

The huge sand city began to take shape. The tower rose from the sand. Worm was crowned King of the Castle. It was a very funny sight.

Everyone was so busy, no one noticed the sea creeping closer and closer.

"Who wants ice cream?" asked Boobela, suddenly stopping digging.

"We do!" yelled all the children. Five wanted strawberry cones, eight wanted chocolate ice cream, and seven vanilla. Most of them wanted chocolate flakes, four wanted chocolate sprinkles, and eight wanted hundreds and thousands. It was quite a lot for Boobela to remember.

"I'll be back soon," she said.

She ran up towards the shops. Because Boobela wanted to make everyone happy, she went from shop to shop to get exactly what the children wanted. Some shops had long queues. Finally, she was finished.

In each hand she held a large box filled with ice cream cones. Delighted, she ran towards the sand city.

Suddenly, she stopped. All she could see was a large stretch of water. Not even the tower was visible. Boobela was sure she was looking in the wrong place. A sandcastle as big as that couldn't just disappear. She ran along the beach, but there was nothing.

Boobela saw Cheryl and Simon. She ran up to them.

"Where's our castle?" she asked breathlessly.

And then "Where's Worm?"

"The tide came in," said Simon. "It covered the castle."

"The tide?" asked Boobela.

"The sea comes in and goes out twice a day," explained Simon.

"How long is it in for?" asked Boobela, feeling very scared.

"The tide is always moving," said Simon. "But the castle was near the highest point. So it shouldn't take long. Maybe an hour."

"An hour!" Boobela cried in panic. "What about Worm? Did someone take him?"

Boobela looked more closely at Cheryl. She could see Cheryl had been crying.

"I tried to get him," said Cheryl. "When the water got up to the city walls. But he wasn't there . . . I looked *everywhere*. I could only find his hat." She offered it to Boobela.

Boobela took the cowboy hat and looked at it. She felt like crying too. But she didn't want to upset Cheryl more.

"I'm sure he's OK," she said bravely. "Show me where the castle was. Then you can give out all these ice creams."

"Are you *sure* he's all right?" asked Cheryl, anxiously.

Boobela nodded. She was so full of feeling she didn't want to speak in case she started to cry.

Simon and Cheryl pointed to where the castle had been. Boobela gave them the boxes of ice creams. They ran off to hand them out.

Boobela cried out to the sea, "Worm, where are you?"

There was no reply. Boobela ran and put her head in the water where Simon and Cheryl had indicated. All she could see was the sand rippling under the waves, as if no castle had ever been.

Boobela left the water and sat on the sand, her head in her hands. She couldn't believe she'd left Worm in danger. She'd been careless because she was so excited about her new friends.

Boobela remembered the tingle she'd felt in her hands when she'd wished the gardener well. They weren't tingling now. Where is the magic in me? Boobela thought. I need it now to find Worm!

She looked at the water. It was further away. The tide was starting to retreat. It seemed to take for ever, but each wave grew more distant, and she could see more and more sand.

Soon the area Simon and Cheryl had indicated was exposed and the sand started to dry out. Boobela ran up and down the beach, shouting,

"Worm! Worm!"

There was no answer.

Then, from where the castle had been, Boobela saw some movement under the sand. She ran towards the spot.

A large lugworm peeked out into the air. It wasn't Worm. Boobela's heart fell. The lugworm crawled slowly out into the sand. Then another head stuck out into the air.

"There you are, pardner," said a familiar voice.

"Worm!" shouted Boobela. "You're all right!"
She could hardly contain herself.

Worm looked at her warily. "No kissing," he
warned.

"I feel like eating you up I'm so happy."

Worm turned to go back into the hole.

"Just joking," she said.

"Just joking," he said as he faced Boobela again.

Boobela slid open Worm's matchbox and he
climbed in. She took his cowboy hat out
of her pocket and put it on him.

Cheryl ran up to Boobela. "He's all right!" she yelled, and she gave Boobela's knees a big hug.

Worm turned to the lugworm. "Thanks for rescuing me. I couldn't have got away from the water if you hadn't shown me your tunnel."

"It was my pleasure," said the lugworm, who spoke very slowly and carefully. "We don't often meet our cousins from the garden."

"You should come and visit," said Worm. He pointed at the sand. "I don't know how you can eat this stuff. It tastes rubbish."

Boobela, Cheryl and the lugworm all laughed.

"I have a rucksack full of lovely things to eat," said Boobela. "I don't suppose you feel hungry?"

Cheryl helped Boobela spread out a blanket and they all settled down to a happy picnic lunch.

Red Letter Day

It was the first of the month and a letter had just arrived for Boobela. It was from her mum and dad. Their letters always arrived on the first and were sealed with red wax, just like this one.

Dear Boobela,

We're sorry to hear Granpa is ill and that Gran had to return home. We expect he's all better now and that she's back with you. We hope you didn't get up to too much mischief when she was away! And that you didn't skip your regular baths – we know how much you hate washing!

Why don't they know that your gran still isn't back?

Worm's nose wrinkled as he remembered Boobela's stinky feet.

Do you save all your parents' letters?

Of course! I read them again and again. Especially when I'm missing Mum and Dad, and feel lonely.

We're staying in a small village at the moment. We've set up a laboratory so that we can study the plants we've collected. One of them cured Dad's cold in a day!

These are my favourite letters ...

This river is so wide you can hardly see the other side. It's filled with colourful fish. One school tried to attack our canoe. Perhaps they thought we were a big fish.

Yesterday we found a whole troop of monkeys with red bottoms. They travelled with us for almost a day. Sometimes they seemed to be laughing at us for looking so closely at plants!

What do they say about me?

They don't know about you yet. I just told them I was doing fine without Gran.

They're my parents. I don't tell them everything. I'll definitely tell them about you though. I'll write to them now.

I wouldn't have said you were doing fine.

What will you say?

That you're a little bossy boots and that you're my best friend ever.

Worm thought he could live with that.

Up, Up and Away

Boobela and Worm lay on the grass in their garden. They were watching the clouds drift by. It was a hot, sticky day and they didn't have the energy for a proper adventure.

"That one's a kangaroo," said Boobela, pointing.

"No, it isn't," said Worm. "It's a giant worm-eater."

"No such thing," said Boobela, giggling. Every cloud looked like a giant worm-eater to Worm today.

A balloon drifted by, carrying two children.

"I wish I could go up in a balloon," said Boobela.

"It would have to be as big as a cloud," said Worm, secretly grateful. Worms, he thought, did not belong in the air.

"I think I'll follow them," said Boobela, jumping to her feet. "Maybe they could help me fly. Are you coming?"

"You'll never catch them," said Worm.

Boobela leaned over and offered Worm his matchbox. "Last chance . . ."

Worm took his time crawling in. He hoped the balloon would disappear.

Once Worm was on board, Boobela dashed out of the house and ran along the road. *There* it was!

Boobela ran down one street after another trying to keep the balloon in sight.

"I'm a worm, Boobela. I'm not meant to fly. Birds fly. Birds eat worms."

"Not in my balloon they wouldn't," replied Boobela.

Boobela came to a sudden stop. Ahead was a crowded main street. The pavements were packed with people. The road was full of vehicles of all sorts. There were steam-powered trucks and cars, and a couple of horse-drawn carriages. "Oh, oh," she exclaimed.

Worm breathed a sigh of relief. They couldn't follow the balloon now. "I can't let it get away!" she cried out.

She stepped into the road and, with a short running start, leaped over the first car in her way. The driver, an old woman with very large glasses, was a bit shocked to see a giant eight-year-old landing on the road in front of her. But she recovered quickly and gave a little wave.

Boobela waved back and leaped over the next car, and then a horse-drawn carriage. In the back of the carriage, twin girls wearing identical dresses cheered and waved.

Boobela smiled. This was fun! Sometimes, she thought, being a giant has its advantages.

The steam truck was too big to jump, so Boobela went up on her tiptoes and ran around the side. Then she jumped over two more cars. At last the road ahead was clear. She could still see the balloon in the distance.

"Yes!" shouted Boobela.

"No . . ." said Worm in a little voice. "I don't want to go up in a balloon, Boobela! I'm an earthworm, not an air worm."

Boobela said, "You're my friend, Worm. I'd love you to come with me but if you don't want to, you don't have to. If *I* get a chance to fly, I will."

Worm breathed a sigh of relief. "Thanks, Boobela."

"No problem. Enjoy the scenery . . ."

. . . which was passing by quickly as Boobela raced down the country road. Now they could see other balloons in the sky. They were all coming down in the same place.

"This must be something big!" exclaimed Boobela.

Boobela could see the field where the balloons were landing. She slowed to a walk. Then she left the road and crept into the grass. She lay down and watched the balloonists. She had learned it was best to approach people slowly, once she knew the lie of the land.

Five balloons were coming down. Under each was a basket carrying several children. On the ground was another group of children.

Boobela watched closely. When the balloons got near the ground, one of the children in the basket would throw a rope over the side, and the children below would grab it.

Boobela looked around. At the edge of the field she could see five horse-drawn school carriages. A large sign with colourful balloons had the words "All Counties Balloon Party" painted on it.

Boobela decided it was time. She stood up and walked towards the children. They were so busy working on their balloons, they didn't see her for quite a while. Then, gradually, she saw people stop working and start to point at her. Soon all the balloonists were staring.

"Hi," said Boobela. She smiled and raised her hand in a sign of peace. The balloonists saw her T-shirt with a big flower on it and smiled too.

Boobela sat down. Sitting down made her look less big. And less scary. Soon she was surrounded by children.

The tallest boy approached Boobela. He had on a greasy red overall. "I'm Jacob. And you're . . ."

"Boobela." She pointed to Worm's matchbox. "And this is my friend Worm." She remembered her manners. "We're very pleased to meet you."

"Likewise," said Jacob. "We don't get many visitors your size." Then he looked at her more closely. "You're a kid!" he said in surprise.

Boobela nodded. "I'm eight." With this, the children around Boobela relaxed.

Sophie, a girl with two pigtails like Boobela, started talking to Worm. "I've never seen a worm like you before. You must be very special to have a giant as a friend."

"I think of it the other way around. She must be a very special giant to have me as a friend."

"I can see you're a worm with Attitude." She laughed. "I'm Sophie, by the way. I have a bit of Attitude myself. At least that's what my father says."

Worm liked Sophie. She was direct, like him.

Sophie said to Boobela, "Do you mind if I take Worm and show him around?"

Boobela looked at Worm, who nodded. She handed Worm's matchbox to Sophie. The two went off, chatting away.

Jacob had been joined by Kate, a girl as tall as him. Worm always told Boobela to get right to the point. She did. "Do you think I'm too big to go up in a balloon?"

"You're definitely too big for one of our balloons," Jacob said. "They're designed for three children." He looked around and spotted a small dark girl in the distance. "Nurgul," he called. "Come over here."

Nurgul looked at the ground as she approached. Boobela could tell she was very shy.

"I'm Boobela," she said softly.

Nurgul kept looking at the ground. "I'm Nurgul," she whispered.

"Nurgul, Boobela has a maths problem."

Nurgul suddenly looked up. "What is it?"

"I want to know if I could go up in a balloon."

"You'd need a big one," said Nurgul. Her shyness seemed to have vanished. "I could work out exactly how big."

As Nurgul talked, Boobela noticed that one of the balloons had come loose. It was starting to drift up into the air. No one had noticed because they were looking at her.

Boobela jumped up. Nurgul, Jake, Kate and the other balloonists jumped back, frightened. Boobela started to run. Then the children realised that she was chasing the runaway balloon.

"Grab the basket," they yelled.

The balloon was going higher and higher. Boobela jumped as high as she could. She missed the basket, but noticed a rope trailing below it. She jumped again, even higher, stretched her fingers and . . .

just barely caught the rope.

In a moment Boobela was surrounded by children shouting and laughing. They took the rope from her hand and tied the balloon down properly.

Kate said, "It took us three years to save up for that. It would have been a disaster if we'd lost it."

Nurgul came up. "I had an idea," she said softly.

"Go ahead," encouraged Kate.

"Well, I was thinking," Nurgul began, "about how big a balloon Boobela would need. It would be the size of three of our balloons. And then I thought that if we tied three balloons together, Boobela could fly today."

"That would be a lot of trouble," said Boobela.

"We owe you some trouble," said Jacob. "You saved us a cartload when you caught that runaway balloon."

Kate called all the children together and explained Nurgul's plan. "We'd better make it four balloons," she said. "We won't have time to show Boobela how to fly. Jacob and I will have to go with her to work the balloons."

The children dragged the three biggest balloons to the one Boobela had rescued. Some got ropes and bungee cords and started to tie the baskets together. Others got very long ropes and linked up the balloons.

Sophie saw what was happening. She turned to Worm, "Isn't that great! You and Boobela are going to fly! You must be so happy!"

"I never said I was going to fly!" said Worm.

Sophie laughed. Before he could stop her, she gave him a big kiss. "You are funny. Of course you're going. You're a very brave worm. Boobela would be lost without you."

Worm considered this. Boobela *would* be lost
without him. But he was scared of flying . . . Still,
he didn't want to disappoint Sophie, who thought
he was some kind of worm hero. Which, of course,
he was.

"I'll do it!" he said.

"Of course you will," said Sophie, proudly,
holding the matchbox high up in the air. She ran
towards the balloons.

The children started to fire up the burners.

Kate said to Boobela, "Time to get aboard!"

Boobela stepped into the biggest basket.

Sophie handed Worm's box to Boobela. "You're going to have such a good time," she said to Worm, who had turned a little  green. She tried to kiss him again but Worm quickly ducked into the matchbox to hide.

"No kissing," he said, safe inside the box.

"This is so exciting!" said Boobela. She wondered if her magic had made it all possible. Then she turned to look at what Kate and Jacob were doing. Worm stayed hidden in his matchbox.

Soon they were ready. "Let's cast off," shouted Kate. "It won't be light for much longer."

The children on the ground untied the baskets and the balloons started to lift into the sky. At first the baskets stayed firmly on the ground, and Boobela worried she was too heavy, but then, with a jerk, they lifted off. Boobela lost her balance and held onto the side of the basket.

"That always happens your first time," said Jacob, laughing.

Boobela gazed around in wonder. It was exactly as she'd imagined. No, *better*. She could see all the children who had helped her getting smaller and smaller, and soon the fields around them began to look like stamps.

For a while she just watched in silence. Kate and Jacob moved from basket to basket turning the burners on and off to keep the balloons at a steady height.

"Don't be daft. Come out and look," she said.

"Is it over yet?" came a voice from inside the matchbox. "I'm not coming out until I'm an earthworm again!"

Boobela smiled. "We're coming down now," she said. Kate and Jacob looked at her. Boobela winked and they caught on at once.

"Yes, the ground's coming up fast!" Kate shouted.

"Watch out for the bump!" said Jacob.

Boobela jumped up and down so that the basket shook, just as if they had hit ground.

"We're down," she said to Worm.

"That's a relief!" said the voice from inside the matchbox. Worm stuck his head out and looked around him. "You big fibber!"

"I wanted you to have a look. Isn't it great?"

Worm looked over the edge of the matchbox at the ground below him. "You'll keep the birds away!"

Boobela nodded.

"It's not bad," said Worm, reluctantly. "Is that where we live?" he asked, nodding his head at a city in the distance.

"Yes," said Kate. She looked at the horizon. The sun was beginning to set. "We're going to have to come down," she added, sadly.

"Do we really?" asked Boobela, disappointed.

Kate nodded. "It'll take a while to get down and there are lots of balloons to deflate and pack up."

Kate and Jacob started to open the valves at the top of the balloons, letting the hot air escape. As they did this, the balloons began to sink lower and lower.

Boobela let down the ropes from the baskets, and the children below caught them. Then Jacob and Kate let out the last of the hot air, and the baskets sank to the ground.

"That was wonderful," said Boobela to Kate and Jacob. She turned to all the children around the basket. "Thank you all so much. It was a dream come true."

As the different clubs took down
their balloons and started to pack them,
Boobela said, "I guess I'll never have a chance
to do this again."

"Not true," piped up Nurgul. "We can build a
balloon big enough for you. I've worked it out."

"Would you really do that for me?" asked
Boobela.

"Of course we would!" said Kate.

Boobela was so pleased she picked up Nurgul and lifted her into the air. At first Nurgul was a bit scared. Then Boobela tossed her up high and caught her. Several times. Nurgul shouted with glee.

"That is as much fun as being up in a balloon!"

The sun had almost set before all the balloons were packed up. Boobela and Worm waved goodbye as the different school carriages left the field.

Boobela went home with her new friends. All the way there they talked about how wonderful ballooning was. Worm had a sleep in his matchbox, and dreamed about tunnelling in the solid, safe ground.

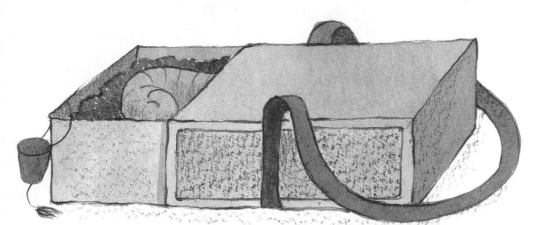

Below my balloon envelope
is a gas burner, like the one
on our cooker. The burners fill
the balloon with hot air. The hotter
the air, the higher we go. But it takes
a lot of hot air to lift me — enough to
fill forty lorries!

I've got two cords inside my
basket. The first makes the
balloon come down slowly. It's
called the parachute cord. When
I pull on it, the hat goes lower
and hot air escapes. When
I let go, it pops back into place.

When I want the balloon to come
down fast, I pull on the rip cord. It
opens the envelope permanently,
and the balloon collapses.

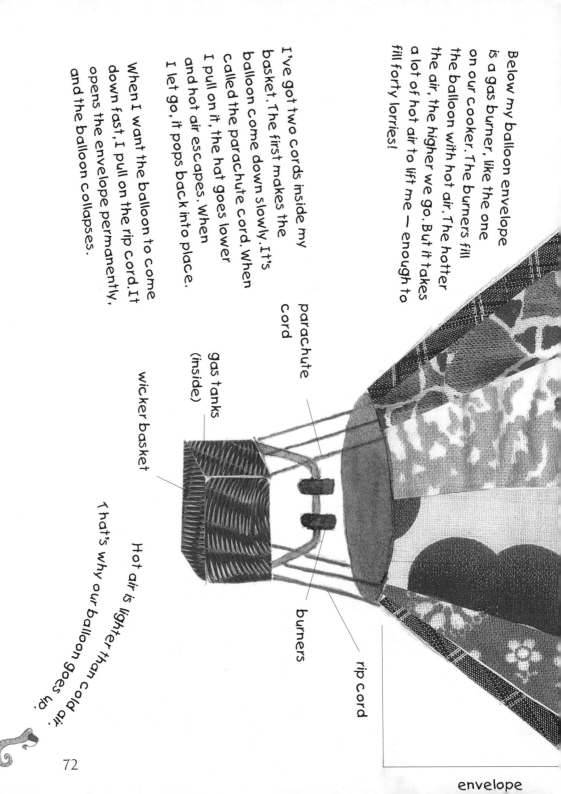

parachute
cord

gas tanks
(inside)

wicker basket

burners

rip cord

Hot air is lighter than cold air.
That's why our balloon goes up.

envelope

72

Out and About in Boobela's World

I love balloons. Travelling
in a balloon is always an
adventure. And you
can go long distances
quickly, when the
wind is right!

panels

parachute valve

To Gran's House

Boobela felt restless. Something was bothering her. She didn't know what.

"Do you want to go for a walk?" she asked Worm. He nodded.

Boobela walked aimlessly along the dark streets. Suddenly she looked up.

"That's where the gardener lives!" she exclaimed. "The one who gave me the mud for your first mud pie!"

Worm remembered the lovely mud pie and licked his lips.

Boobela looked more closely at the house. She could see the gardener dancing with his wife. His movements were smooth and easy. Boobela remembered how her hands had tingled after he had helped her.

"*Was* it magic?" she asked Worm.

"Who could tell you?"

Boobela shook her head.

"Who's the smartest person you know?" Worm persisted.

Boobela thought. "My gran!" she exclaimed. "It's been months since I've seen her. I miss her . . . *That's* what's bothering me!"

Boobela thought about her new balloon, the one the club had made for her. "We could fly my new balloon!"

"*We?*" said Worm sharply.

"I forgot," said Boobela. "You're scared of flying. I'll have to learn to map-read myself. It's just that if I get lost on the way to Gran's house, the balloon will end up in the sea . . . and I can't swim."

Worm raised his eyes towards the sky. "I've already spent a week trying to teach you! You still get lost going around the corner." He sighed heavily. "I'll go with you."

"Really?" asked Boobela.

"Really," said Worm.

• • •

The morning of the flight, Boobela went to her mother's jewellery box and took out her mum's amber necklace. Her mother had sort of said she could borrow it. It was too small to go on her neck, so she wore it as a bracelet.

When they arrived at the launch field Jacob, Kate and Sophie were already there. The new balloon was laid out.

Sophie gave Worm a hat she had knitted to keep him warm. It had "Air Worm" in red letters on it. She took him to the little house Boobela had built for him on the basket. It had a map on the ceiling and a light so that Worm could see where they were going. It also had a little hole in the bottom so Worm could see the ground.

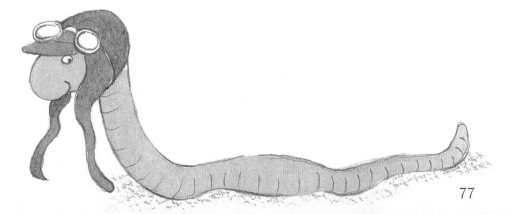

As Sophie put him in the basket, Worm saw
The Look in her eye and knew she was about to
kiss him. He ducked below the soil. 'No kissing,'
he said in a muffled voice.

"Time to go," said Kate. "Have a great trip!"

Jacob untied the rope and the balloon leaped up
into the sky.

In a few moments they were flying north. The
wind blew steadily. Worm gave regular reports on
where they were.

After a while, Worm said, "We should go over the sea in a couple of minutes!"

And sure enough, the land ended and the short stretch of sea began. They could see the small island where Boobela's gran lived just ahead. Boobela glanced at her bracelet. Gran would love it.

"Start going down," said Worm. "See the field with the trees at one end? Land there."

Boobela pulled the parachute hat hard. The balloon started to drop like a stone.

"Not so fast!" yelled Worm.

The basket hit the ground and bounced several times along the field. Boobela pulled the rip cord and the empty balloon collapsed on them.

Boobela climbed out from under the balloon. She opened Worm's house and let him climb into his matchbox.

"Could you make it bumpier next time?" asked Worm sarcastically.

"Sorry," said Boobela. "It all happened a bit fast."

They saw someone running towards them. It was Gran. At first, Boobela was surprised to see her. How did she know they were coming? But then she remembered her Gran always seemed to know things without being told.

Boobela ran towards her, knelt down and gave her a big hug.

"That was a very impressive arrival," said Gran. Worm giggled.

Boobela introduced him. "This is my best pal Worm."

Worm smiled and bowed.

"Where's Granpa?" Boobela asked.

Gran clucked and said he still wasn't well.

It was then Boobela noticed. The necklace was gone! It had come off during the landing.

What would her mother say?

"I've lost the necklace!" she cried out.

Gran looked at her.

"It's Mum's. I took it to show you. I've got to find it!"

It was already getting dark. Because the basket had bounced three times there was a huge area to search. It was covered with plants.

Gran took Boobela's hand. "It won't go anywhere tonight," she said in a warm voice. "We'll find it in the morning."

Worm touched Boobela on the neck. "She's right," he said. "Let's look for it tomorrow."

Gran helped pack up the balloon and soon

Boobela and Worm were nice and cosy in
Gran's barn house. Granpa joined them for
dinner. It was chicken soup, Boobela's
favourite. Worm had his first taste of the
local soil.

After dinner, Granpa went back to bed.
Gran asked Boobela what had brought her
and Worm such a long way.

Boobela told her Gran she had missed
her. Gran gave her a big hug.

"And your hands . . ." Worm prompted.

Hesitantly, Boobela told Gran what had happened with the gardener. She didn't want Gran to think she was telling stories.

Gran listened seriously. "Did your hands get hot?"

Boobela nodded. Gran sat in silence for a while. Boobela was nervous. She thought she might have said something wrong.

"My hands started to tingle when I was your age. When my best friend fell and got hurt," said Gran.

"Did you make her better?" asked Boobela.

Gran nodded.

"Is that magic?" asked Worm.

"Of a sort," said Gran. "Magic isn't spells and abracadabra and hocus pocus. Magic is in your heart and in your mind."

Boobela told Gran how Worm had been caught by the tide and how she'd wanted to find him but her hands hadn't tingled at all.

Gran was quiet again. "You're at the start of a long journey," said Gran. "Tomorrow I'll teach you to dowse. That will help you to use your mind better."

"What's dowsing?" Worm asked.

Gran thought for a minute. "Dowsing is a way of looking for things."

By now, Boobela and Worm were too tired to listen any further. Gran tucked them in and they were asleep in seconds.

After breakfast the next day, Gran took them out into her garden. She held out a large, Y-shaped branch.

Boobela took it. "What's this for?" she asked.

"In dowsing," said Gran, "you use a stick or a couple of metal rods to help you look for something."

Worm didn't understand. "A stick can't show you where something is!"

"It's not the stick. It's your mind. Everyone knows much more than they think. Your mind uses the stick to show you what you need to know."

Gran looked at Boobela closely. "Gently does it," she said. "You're holding the branch like it will run away."

Boobela let go. It fell to the ground.

"Not that loosely," said Gran, laughing.

"What's supposed to happen?" Boobela asked.

"Perhaps nothing," said Gran. "We're trying to find the right tool for you. I use the hazel so I thought I'd try that first. Ask it for a 'yes'."

"Ask the branch?" asked Boobela, feeling a bit silly.

Gran nodded. Boobela silently asked the branch to say "yes". Nothing happened.

Gran took the branch and handed her two L-shaped rods – each made from a large, metal coat hanger. Boobela felt a bit disappointed. "They don't look very magical," she said.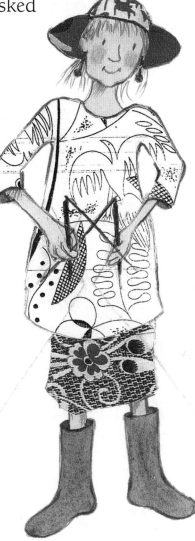

"The magic isn't in them, love. It's in *you*," said Gran. "Hold them in front of you and ask them for a 'no'."

Boobela did the same as before. But this time, to her surprise, the rods immediately swung together and crossed over.

"The rods it is," said Gran.

"I didn't *do* anything, Gran!" protested Boobela.

"Exactly," said Gran. "You're learning. Ask them to find the barn."

Boobela pointed the rods towards it.

"No!" said Gran forcefully. "You don't point them. Just hold them loosely and let them find the barn."

"But it's right here!" said Boobela.

"If you don't learn how to use them properly to find things you can see, you won't be able to find things you can't see," said Gran.

"Like Worm when he was under the water?"

Gran nodded. "Just keep your mind empty and think of the cottage."

Boobela tried holding the rods very loosely and asked, "Where is the barn?" After a few long minutes, they moved slowly and pointed at it.

Gran took a small bottle out of her pocket.
She showed it to Boobela. "You're going to
look for this," she said. "With your eyes
closed." She blindfolded Boobela and
hid the bottle.

Several times Boobela thought
she'd found it. She asked Worm.
He didn't say anything. Then
the rods crossed over
strongly. She removed
the blindfold. There it
was! She felt pleased.

Finally, Gran asked
Worm to go deep underground.

"Is Boobela supposed to
find me?" asked Worm.

Gran nodded.

Worm thought for a moment and then disappeared into the soil. He decided to make it difficult for Boobela by hiding underground right near the stone wall fence.

After half an hour Gran asked Boobela to find Worm. Boobela walked around the centre of the garden. The rods didn't cross at all.

"It's not working," she said.

"Have you looked everywhere?" asked Gran.

Boobela looked around the garden. She realised she hadn't gone near the walls. She closed her eyes and started walking again. Suddenly the rods crossed! She dropped a stone to mark the spot.

"I think Worm is under here," she said. Then she shouted, "Worm! Come straight up."

She waited and waited. Then a little head came out from the ground, right next to her stone. Worm looked at the stone, then at Boobela.

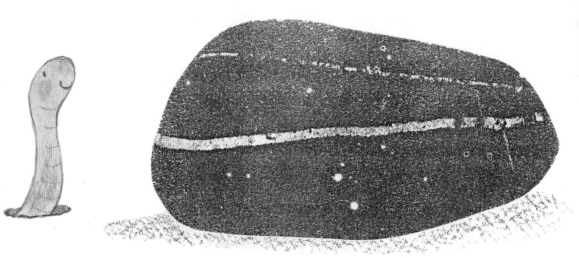

"You did it!" said Worm, pleased.

Boobela jumped up and down with excitement. She'd never lose Worm again!

"Time for dinner," said Gran.

Boobela realised she'd been dowsing for hours!

Over dinner, Boobela said, "When are we going to find the necklace?"

"Tomorrow," said Gran. "*You're* going to find it."

The next morning, Gran took Boobela out into the field where the balloon had landed. "Keep a picture of it in your mind," she said. "And just wander where your feet take you. I'm going to do some gardening."

Boobela walked around, looking at the ground.

"*Don't look!*" said Worm. "The rods will find it, just like they found me."

Boobela stood still and relaxed. When she felt a bit dreamy, she let her feet wander where they wanted to. Suddenly the rods crossed, quite

violently. Boobela was shocked. She looked down
and saw a green mass of plants.

"Let me look," said Worm. She knelt and put him
down. Then she picked carefully through the leaves.
After a few minutes she got down to the soil. There
was the necklace – with Worm sitting on top.

"I did it. I found it!" she shouted.

"Well done!" said Worm. "Let's show Gran."

They found Gran working in
the garden and showed her the
necklace. Gran smiled and nodded. "You've
worked hard," she said. She looked up at the trees.
The wind had changed direction.

"You'll have to head back tomorrow," she said.

Boobela's face fell. "I don't want to!" she protested.
"We're having a great time!"

Worm nodded.

"I'm enjoying this too," said Gran. "But too
much excitement isn't good for Granpa. I'll be
seeing you again soon enough," she said,
mysteriously.

"What do you mean?" asked Boobela.

"That would be telling," said Gran.

"That's not fair," said Boobela and Worm together.

"You have a gift," said Gran. "It will take more than two days to develop it." She wouldn't say anything further until she tucked Boobela into bed. "I'm pleased you've found such a good friend," she whispered.

"So am I," said Boobela. Boobela and Worm both dreamed of the magic rods and what fun they would have with them when they got home.